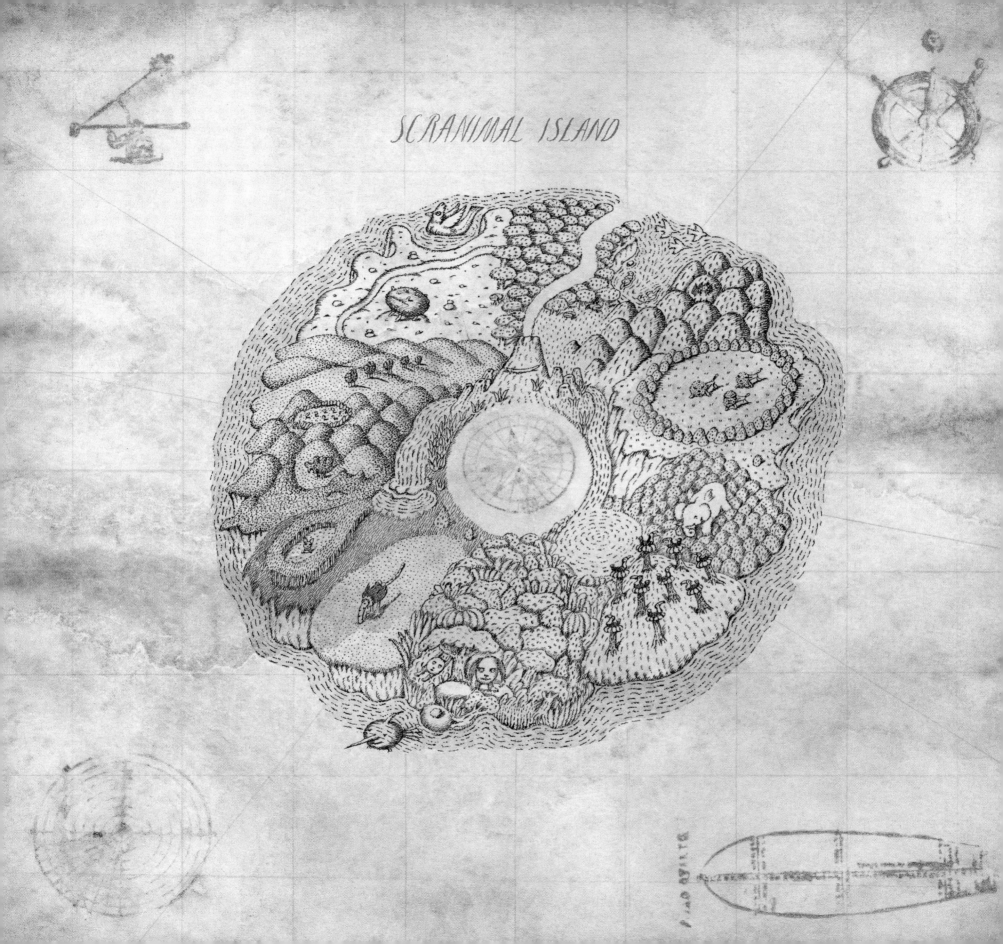

Scranimals

POEMS BY JACK PRELUTSKY
PICTURES BY PETER SÍS

GREENWILLOW BOOKS
An Imprint of HarperCollinsPublishers

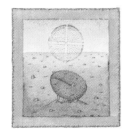

TO AVA WEISS,
FOR BEAUTIFUL BOOKS
— J. P.

FOR GINNY MOORE KRUSE
AND EVERYONE AT THE
COOPERATIVE CHILDREN'S BOOK CENTER
— P. S.

Scranimals
Text copyright © 2002 by Jack Prelutsky
Illustrations copyright © 2002 by Peter Sís
All rights reserved.
Printed in the United States of America.
www.harperchildrens.com

Black line art is combined with watercolors for the full-color illustrations.
The typeface is Gill Sans.

Library of Congress Cataloging-in-Publication Data

Prelutsky, Jack.
Scranimals / by Jack Prelutsky ; illustrated by Peter Sís.
    p.   cm.
"Greenwillow Books."
ISBN 0-688-17819-7 (trade). ISBN 0-688-17820-0 (lib. bdg.)
1. Nonsense-verses, American. 2. Children's poetry, American.
[1. Animals—Poetry. 2. Humorous poetry. 3. American poetry.]
I. Sís, Peter, ill. II. Title.   PS3566.R36 S37 2002
811'.54—dc21   2001023620

First Edition 10 9 8 7 6 5 4 3 2 1

CONTENTS

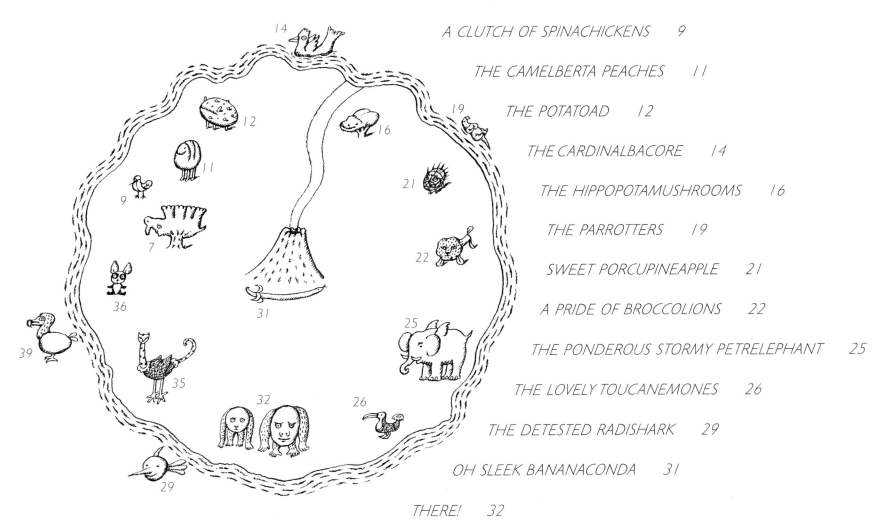

We're sailing to Scranimal Island,

It doesn't appear on most maps.

The PARROTTERS float on the tide there,

The STORMY PETRELEPHANT flaps.

We may find a rare OSTRICHEETAH,

There's never been one in a zoo.

We're sailing to Scranimal Island—

You're welcome to come along too.

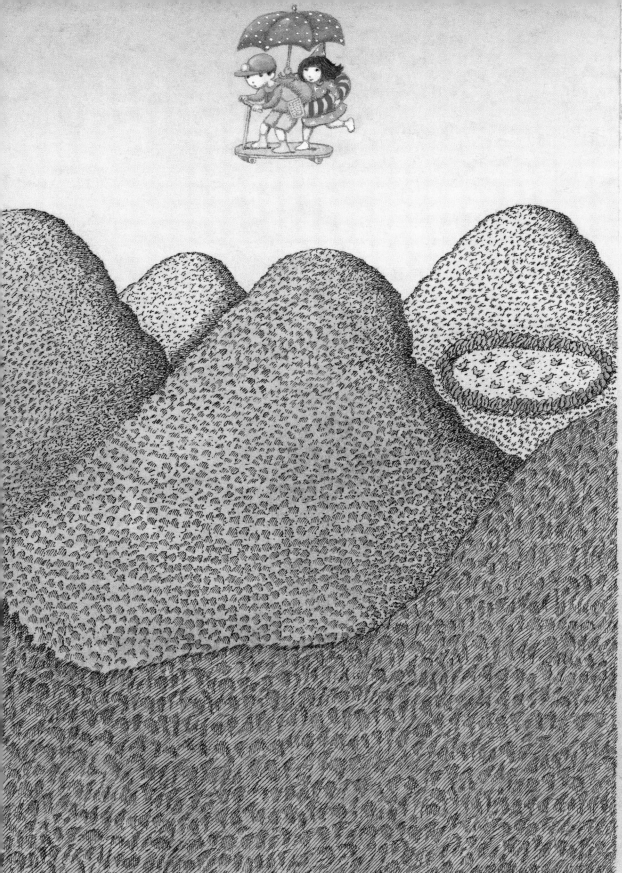

Oh beautiful RHINOCEROSE,
So captivating, head to toes,
So aromatic, toes to head,
Enchantress of the flower bed,
Your blossoms cheer us every morn,
And we adore your tail and horn.
You soothe the eyes, delight the nose,
Most glorious RHINOCEROSE.

rye-NOSS-ur-oze

A clutch of SPINACHICKENS
Is fussing in the yard,
They peck their meager pickings,
Their lives are dull and hard.
Except for paltry feathers,
They're mostly leafy green,
Their heads are smooth as leather,
Their brains are not too keen.

Some say that they're distasteful,
While others think they're sweet,
They're never very graceful,
They wilt at signs of heat.
They mill about all morning
Upon their scrawny legs,
Then cluck a single warning
And lay their turquoise eggs.

spin-itch-ICK-inz

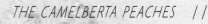

On the sunbaked, barren beaches,
Courtly CAMELBERTA PEACHES
Gather into stately bands
To patrol the burning sands.
Some are yellow, some are green,
Most are sort of in-between,
All have puffy, plump physiques,
Knobby knees, and fuzzy cheeks.

All have humpy, bumpy backs,
Stocked with water, juice, and snacks,
So the creatures never need
Wonder where to drink or feed.
By the salty sea they stride,
Never noticing the tide,
Up and down the sifting sands . . .
CAMELBERTA caravans.

CAM-ull-BURR-tuh

On a bump beside a road
Sits a lowly POTATOAD,
Obviously unaware
Of its own existence there.

On its coarse and warty hide,
It has eyes on every side,
Eyes that fail, apparently,
To take note of what they see.

It does not move, it does not think,
It does not eat, it does not drink,
It does not hear or taste or touch...
The POTATOAD does not do much.

The day is hot, the ground is parched,
And yet it sits as if it's starched.
To pose immobile by a road
Suffices for the POTATOAD.

poe-tay-TOAD

The CARDINALBACORE
Has a face entirely red.
Its busy wings are sore
From holding up its head.
It hovers on the brink,
Its existence isn't fair,
Its tail flops in the drink,
But its top stays in the air.

It simply cannot let
Its own bottom pull it down.
If it got entirely wet,
It would definitely drown.
Yet the CARDINALBACORE
Seems undaunted by the fact
That its life is nothing more
Than a full-time circus act.

car-din-AL-buh-core

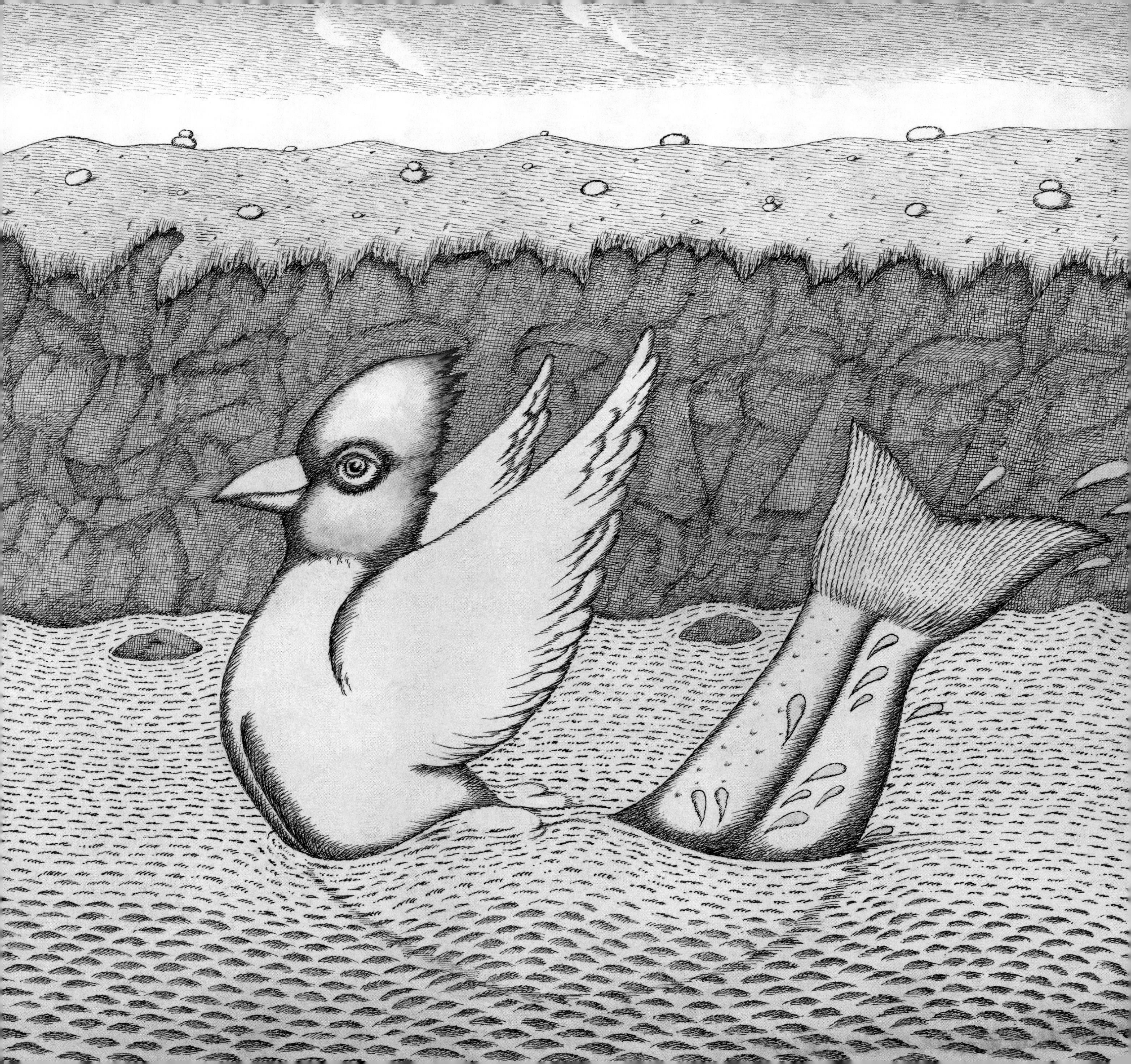

The **HIPPOPOTAMUSHROOMS**
Cannot wander very far.
How fortunate they're satisfied
Precisely where they are.
They feel no need to travel,
They're forever at their ease,
Relaxing on the forest floor
Beneath the shady trees.

The **HIPPOPOTAMUSHROOMS**
Suffer from deficient grace,
And their tubby, blobby bodies
Tend to take up too much space.
But they compensate with manners
For the things they lack in style...
They are models of politeness,
And they always wear a smile.

hip-uh-pot-uh-MUSH-rooms

The PARROTTERS lie
On their backs in the sea,
Calling to cormorants,
Yapping at auks.
They cannot stop prattling,
Though most would agree
That no one pays heed
When a PARROTTER talks.

PAA-rot-urz

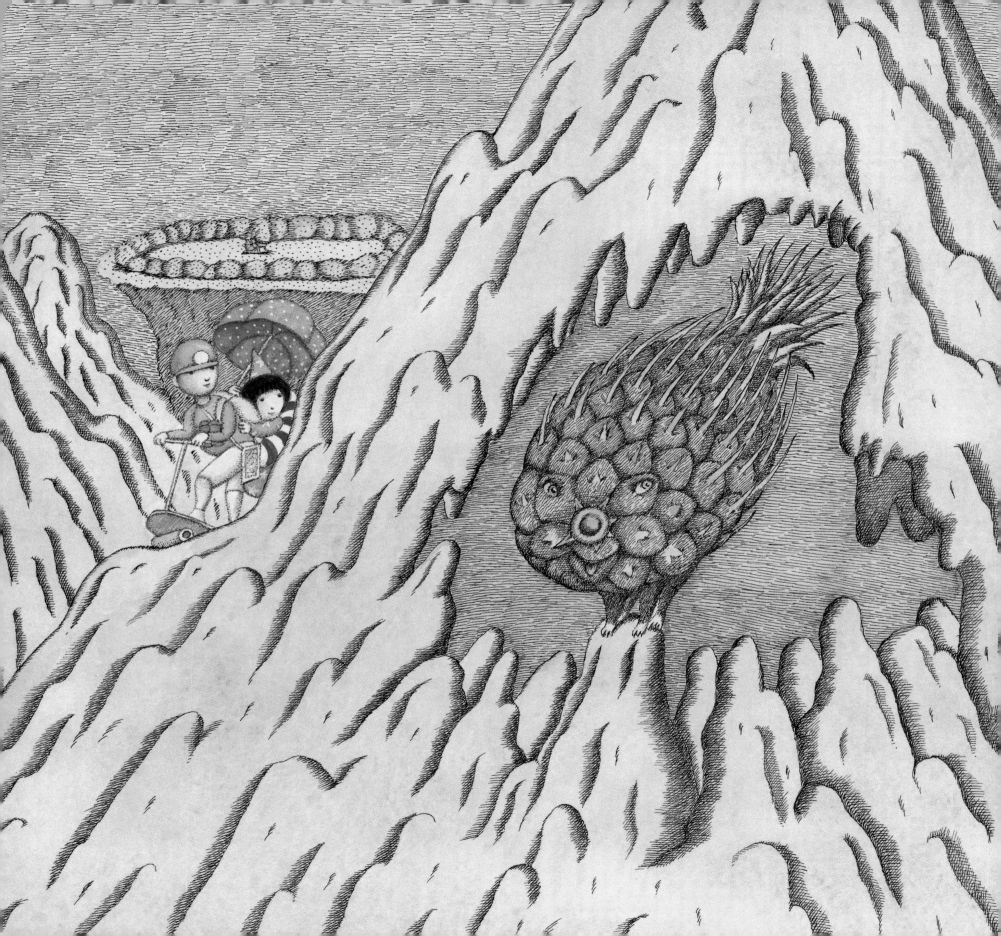

Sweet PORCUPINEAPPLE,
Unflappable chap,
You happily amble
All over the map.
Sharp prickles protect
Your subtropical hide,
Not many could chew you,
Not many have tried.

Your spirits are high,
And your worries are few,
You go where you go,
And you do what you do.
A pointed example
Of perfect design,
Sweet PORCUPINEAPPLE,
Your life is divine.

por-cue-pie-NAP-ul

A pride of BROCCOLIONS
Has assembled in the grass,
Paying scrupulous attention
To the creatures ranging past.
Then an ANTELOPETUNIA
Moves directly into view,
And the chase begins in earnest,
And they all know what to do.

They are beasts of regal bearing
In their coats of green and gold.
They are fierce and prepossessing,
They are cunning, they are bold.
Soon their chosen victim stumbles,
For despite its nimble gait,
Its pursuers overtake it
And consign it to its fate.

With adroitness and precision
They dispatch their fallen prey,
And that ANTELOPETUNIA
Will not bloom another day.
Then that pride of BROCCOLIONS,
Having hunted, having fed,
Growls and yawns in satisfaction
And goes noisily to bed.

brock-uh-LIE-unz
an-till-oh-puh-TUNE-yuh

The ponderous STORMY PETRELEPHANT
Is futilely trying to fly.
Its efforts are clearly irrelevant,
One look and it's plain to see why.
Its wings are too small to support it,
They're patently only for show,
And so it is constantly thwarted . . .
Up isn't a place it can go.

It hasn't a hope of succeeding,
It's destined to wander the plains,
Which, given its bulk and its breeding,
Is where we prefer it remains.
The STORMY PETRELEPHANT's failures
Relieve us of absolute dread.
We love it in fields of azaleas—
We'd hate if it soared overhead.

peh-TRELL-uh-fint

The lovely TOUCANEMONES,
Profuse upon the hills,
Display their gaudy petals
And their multicolored bills.
They revel in the sunshine,
They rejoice to feel the breeze,
And every drop of rain delights
The TOUCANEMONES.

The lovely TOUCANEMONES
Are quite a noisy bunch.
They chatter when they waken
And continue well past lunch.
If you should pet their blossoms,
Tantalizing to the touch,
They're apt to nip your fingers,
Though they will not nip them much.

At times the TOUCANEMONES
May flap their wings awhile,
As if to rise into the skies,
But that is not their style.
They're clearly underqualified
To soar above the trees—
An earthbound life's the limit
For the TOUCANEMONES.

two-can-EM-uh-neez

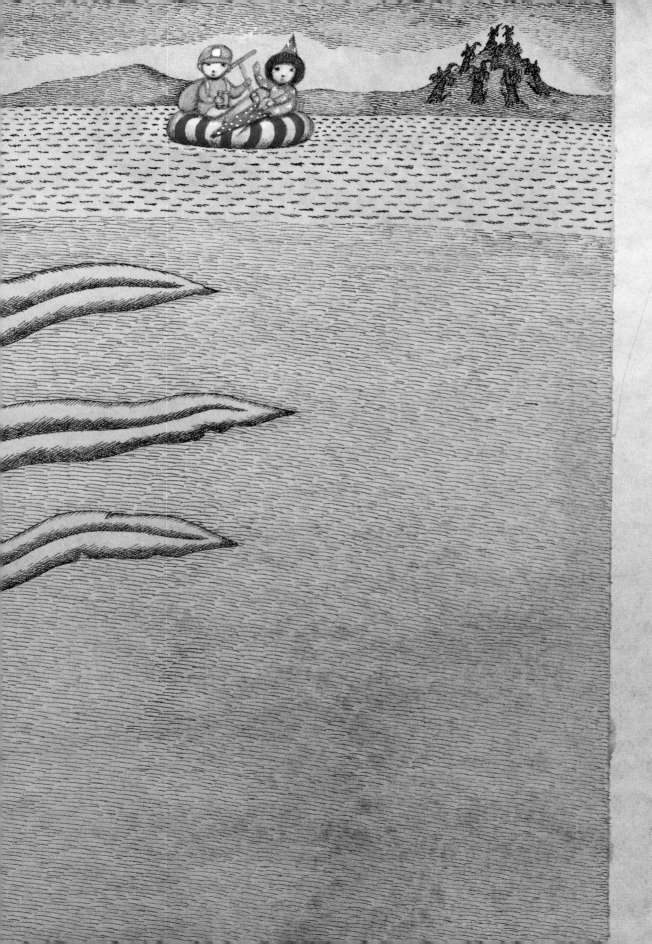

In the middle of the ocean,
In the deep deep dark,
Dwells a monstrous apparition,
The detested RADISHARK.
It's an underwater nightmare
That you hope you never meet,
For it eats what it wants,
And it always wants to eat.

Its appalling, bulbous body
Is astonishingly red,
And its fangs are sharp and gleaming
In its huge and horrid head,
And the only thought it harbors
In its small but frightful mind,
Is to catch you and to bite you
On your belly and behind.

It is ruthless, it is brutal,
It swims swiftly, it swims far,
So it's guaranteed to find you
Almost anywhere you are.
If the RADISHARK is near you,
Pray the beast is fast asleep
In the middle of the ocean
In the dark dark deep.

RAD-ish-ark

Oh sleek **BANANACONDA,**
You longest long long fellow,
How sinuous and sly you are,
How slippery, how yellow.

You slither on your belly,
And you slither on your chin.
You're only unappealing
As you shed your slinky skin.

buh-na-nuh-CON-duh

There! Cavorting through the jungle
In a sea of brilliant green,
Please observe the MANGORILLA
And ORANGUTANGERINE.
They are racing, they are sparring,
Playing leapfrog, tag, and catch,
And in every competition
They are one another's match.

Now the MANGORILLA dances
On a verdant, mossy bed,
While his acrobatic playmate
Swings in branches overhead.
We feel privileged to view them,
They are rare and seldom seen . . .
The enormous MANGORILLA,
The ORANGUTANGERINE.

man-guh-RILL-uh
uh-RANG-uh-tan-jur-EEN

Behold the OSTRICHEETAH,
A blur that rushes past,
There is not a creature fleeter,
Not a creature quite as fast.
It swiftly covers distance,
Never slackening its pace.
Throughout its whole existence,
It has yet to lose a race.

With fur and feathers flying,
It hurtles on and then,
Somehow, not even trying,
Accelerates again.
But when it tires of running,
It doesn't simply stand.
Though quick, it's far from cunning—
Its head goes in the sand.

ah-stri-CHEE-tuh

On a certain mountain meadow,
If you're silent, if you're still,
You may spy a single yellow,
Black, and white PANDAFFODIL.
You may even hear it yawning
If the morning's just begun,
Watch its petals slowly open
To embrace the rising sun.

You may see it soon meander
To a stand of tall bamboo,
Pluck a succulent example,
And commence to chomp and chew.
It may plop upon its belly,
Flop upon its downy back,
Turn an amiable cartwheel,
And continue with its snack.

You may see it fold its petals
When the sun sinks overhead,
And in languorous contentment
Trundle homeward and to bed.
You may never see another
Gentle, shy PANDAFFODIL,
Even on that mountain meadow,
Though you're silent, though you're still.

pan-DAFF-uh-dill

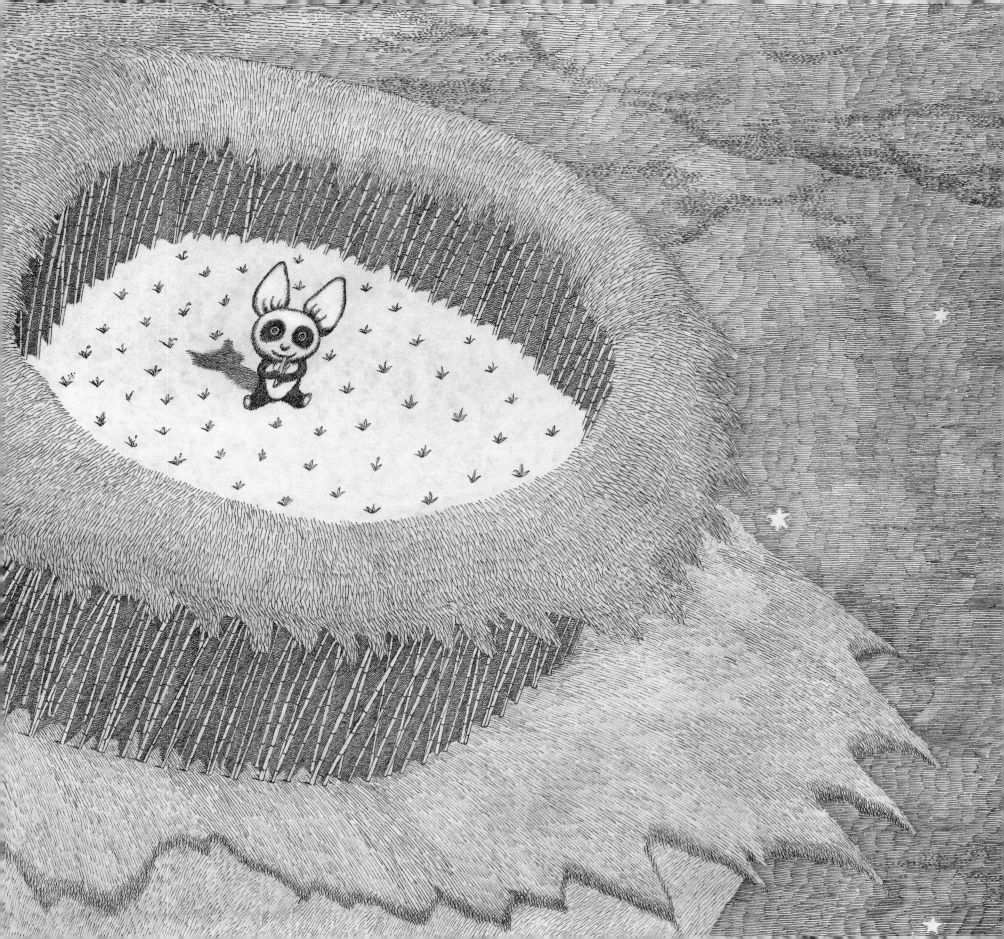

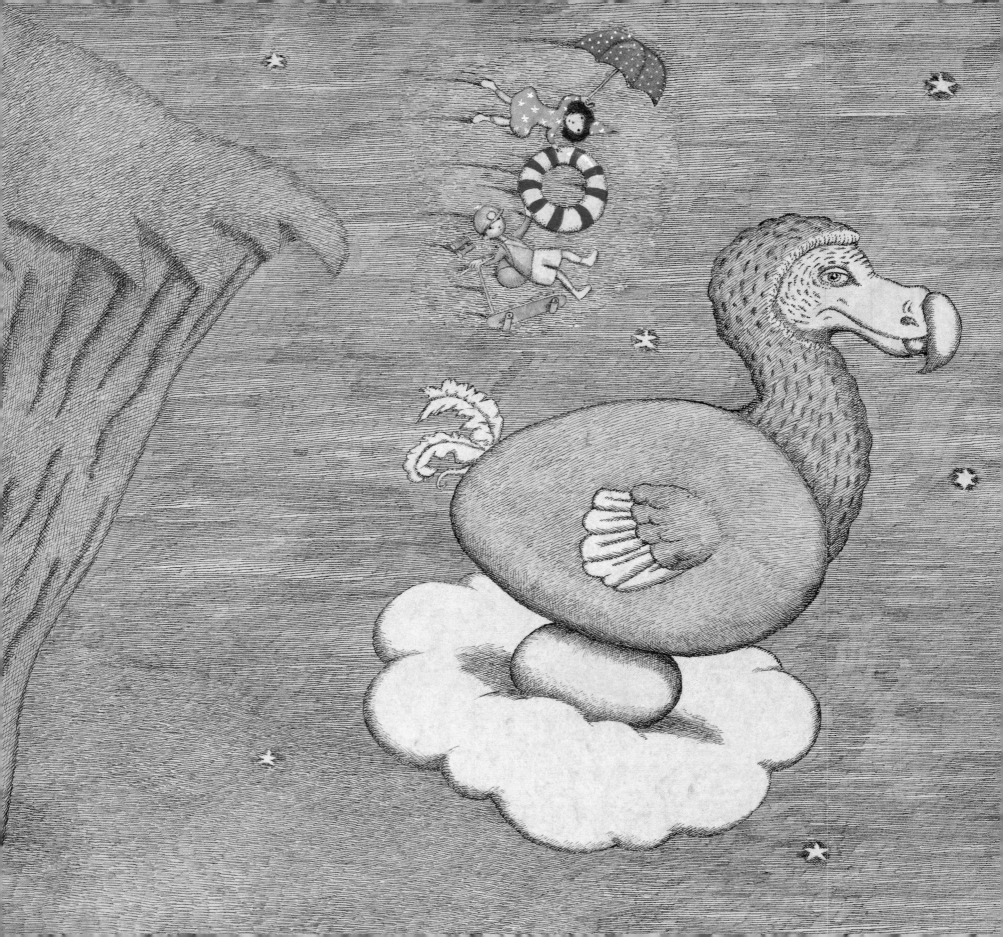

Poor AVOCADODOS,
Ungainly and green,
You're gone from today's
Biological scene.
Your craniums held
But a bit of brain,
Explaining in part
Why you didn't remain.

You never were fast,
And you never were strong,
It's hardly surprising
You couldn't last long.
A fruit and a fowl
Inexplicably linked,
Poor AVOCADODOS,
You're sadly extinct.

ah-vuh-ca-DOE-doze

We've journeyed to Scranimal Island,
Where magical creatures are found,
Where AVOCADODOS still flourish,
And green SPINACHICKENS abound.
We've seen a PANDAFFODIL dining,
A PORCUPINEAPPLE at play.
Perhaps there is more to discover—
We'd like to return there someday.

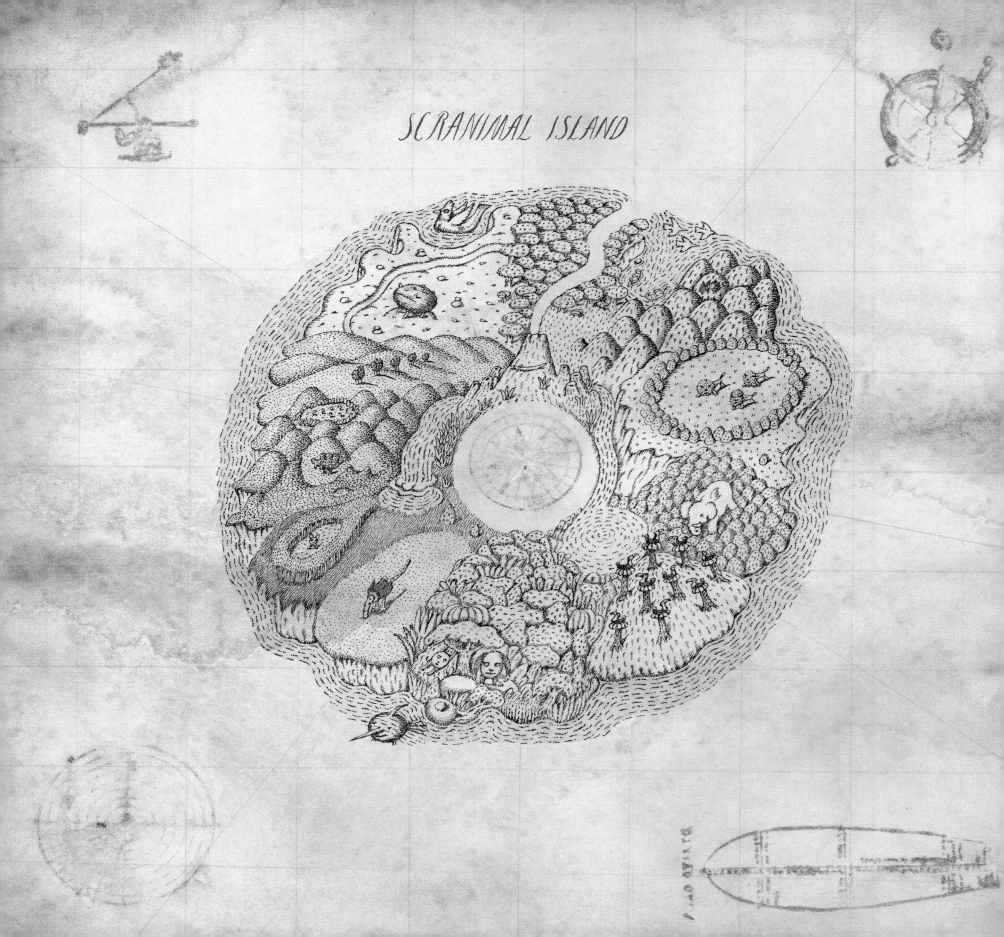

SCRANIMAL ISLAND